Volume 1

All-Time Favourite

FAIRY TALES

5-IN-1

Retold by Ken Spillman

Art by Beth Parrocha

SCHOLASTIC
New York Toronto London Auckland
Sydney New Delhi Hong Kong

Dr Ken Spillman is the author of more than 50 books including the internationally popular Jake series. Based in Australia, Ken travels frequently and has spoken to more than 70,000 children in the past four years. He is a long-time advocate for writers and writing in the Asian region and actively supports organisations connecting marginalised children with the world of stories. For more information, visit: www.kenspillman.com.

Beth Parrocha is a children's book illustrator who loves colour. She has more than 50 children's books to her name. Come play with her as she brings your favourite book characters to life.

Published by Scholastic India Pvt. Ltd.
A subsidiary of Scholastic Inc., New York, 10012 (USA).
Publishers since 1920, with international operations in Canada,
Australia, New Zealand, the United Kingdom, India, and Hong Kong.

For information regarding permission, write to:
Scholastic India Pvt. Ltd.
A-27, Ground Floor, Bharti Sigma Centre
Infocity-1, Sector 34, Gurgaon 122001 (India)

ISBN-13: 978-93-5103-700-2

First edition: December 2014

This reprint edition: April 2025

Printed in India at MicroPrints India, New Delhi

CONTENTS

Sleeping Beauty

A very long time ago, a King and Queen were blessed with a daughter. In celebration, they asked all the fairies of the kingdom to become the Princess's godmothers. It was customary for fairy godmothers to offer special gifts to the newborn, and the seven fairies were delighted when a feast was arranged for the announcement of their seven special gifts.

To everyone's surprise, an eighth fairy also came to the feast. She was extremely old. No one had seen her for fifty years, so the King and Queen—and even the other fairies—had imagined she was dead. The old fairy was upset that she had not been named as a godmother to the Princess, nor even invited to the feast. Even though she was asked to take a place at the table of honour, she could not forgive them. She became even angrier when she learned that the King and Queen were

unable to give their unexpected guest the same gift of gold, diamonds and rubies that had been prepared for each of the other fairies.

One of the other fairies grew worried that the eighth fairy might take out her anger on the baby girl. When the time came to announce their gifts, this young fairy ensured she was last in line. Only then, she thought, could she reverse any nasty spells by the bad-tempered fairy.

The first of the fairies gave the Princess the gift of beauty, promising the King and Queen that their daughter would be the fairest maiden in all the land. The next fairy promised that the Princess would have a heart and mind as pure as an angel. The third fairy gave the child unlimited intelligence, while the fourth pledged that she would sparkle in conversation. The fifth fairy offered grace of movement—for the King and Queen had always dreamed of a daughter who would shine at palace dances—while the sixth gave the Princess a talent for singing and playing music.

It was now the turn of the bitter old fairy. The younger godmothers noticed she was shaking with meanness and spite. Even so, the evil she spoke shocked them.

'I declare, Your Majesties, that the Princess will one day prick her finger with a needle, and that the wound will cause her death as sure as night follows day.'

The Queen shrieked in horror and the King trembled. All present, except the wicked old fairy, shed tears—even the seventh young fairy, who knew she did not have the power to undo such a powerful spell. She thought long and hard, wondering what she could do to save the Princess from her terrible fate. Finally, she spoke.

'My dear King and Queen, I cannot repair what my elder godmother has done. I can help just a little. If your daughter should prick herself with a needle, she shall not die of the wound. Instead of dying, she will fall into a deep sleep. She will not open her eyes for a hundred years—and even then, only if a Prince shall wake her.'

Hoping to prevent the tragedy that had been foretold by the old fairy, the King announced a palace ban on both needles and pins. Years passed, and the gifts of the good fairy godmothers were there for all to see in the young Princess. She was a charming, bright and beautiful young woman, with talents unequalled across many kingdoms.

One day, with the King and Queen gone to one of their country houses, the Princess explored parts of the palace she had never yet seen. There were servants' quarters, storerooms, pantries and a kitchen. Up the stairs she ran, from one room to the other. Too soon she came to a little garret, where an old woman sat alone with her spinning wheel, sewing box and embroidery.

'What are you doing?' asked the Princess.

'I am spinning, my pretty child,' croaked the woman. She seemed surprised to have a visitor, having worked alone and forgotten in her garret for more years than she could remember.

'Oh, how lovely this is!' exclaimed the Princess, picking up some embroidery. 'How do you do it?'

Having no knowledge of needles, the Princess took hold of the cloth carelessly. As the old fairy godmother had foretold, she pricked a finger. Immediately, she collapsed. The woman had not been told of the evil curse, so her first thought was that the Princess had fainted at the sight of her own blood. When her attempts to revive her were unsuccessful, she hurried downstairs and raised the alarm.

The King and Queen returned to the castle to find their

precious daughter lying peacefully in her chamber, surrounded by weeping servants. They feared that she was dead before her soft breathing and rosy cheeks told them otherwise. The King remembered the prediction of the old fairy and knew with terrible certainty what had happened.

Heartbroken, the King and Queen sent for the kind fairy godmother who had spoken last at the feast after the Princess was born. Without her fast thinking, they realised, their beautiful daughter would now be dead, not sleeping. They hoped against hope that the good fairy might help them again.

'Your Majesties,' the fairy godmother said, 'as much as it pains me to say this, only a Prince can wake her, a hundred years from now. The kindest thing I can do is make sure she does not wake to find a castle full of strangers.'

With that, she touched the King and Queen with her magic wand. The royal couple felt instantly sleepy, and realised what the fairy had done. They went to their chamber and tucked themselves into bed.

'You will wake when the Sleeping Beauty is woken by her Prince,' the fairy told them.

Before leaving, she also cast a spell on the loyal servants of the household, putting them all under the blanket of a deep sleep. Outside, the fairy godmother waved her wand again. A dense forest grew up at astonishing speed and hid the castle from view, for the fairy wished to protect the Princess from the curiosity of strangers.

Stories of the lovely Princess who had been transformed into a Sleeping Beauty were passed from fathers and mothers to sons and daughters, and from kingdom to faraway kingdom. To many, the story seemed no more than the work of a great imagination. Yet there were others who suspected that some of it, at least, might be true.

Exactly a hundred years after the Princess pricked her finger, the son of a King from a nearby land was out hunting with his men. Finding a dense forest that, he was told, no person in living memory had entered—and curious to see what birds and animals lived among the thorns and brambles—he ordered his men to cut through the undergrowth. The Prince raised his own sword and was astonished to see a path open up magically before his eyes. At the end of the path, he saw a castle. Moss grew upon its steps, wild creepers covered

its walls, and birds had nested in its every nook and cranny. Remembering the story of the Sleeping Beauty, the Prince felt his heart race. He ordered his men to wait, and went inside.

Everything the Prince saw might have frozen his blood with terror. All was silent. Bodies were stretched out everywhere, seemingly lifeless. When the Prince heard guards and servants snoring, however, he realised that they were only asleep. He passed through rooms with ladies and gentlemen all asleep, and at last came to the chamber of the Princess. There he saw the loveliest sight he had ever looked upon—the Sleeping Beauty of legend, a Princess whose beauty shone even brighter than the long-ago day she had closed her eyes. The Prince approached, trembling and admiring, and knelt beside her. At that moment, the enchantment ended. The Sleeping Beauty awoke, gazing at him with great tenderness.

'Is it you, Prince?' she said. 'I have waited long for you to come.'

The Prince was delighted by her words and overcome by the fondness in her voice. 'My Princess,' he blurted, 'I did not know it, but I have been looking for you, waiting for this day.'

By now the servants of the palace had woken and were

once again busy with their daily tasks. The King and Queen were also awake, and they dashed to the splendid chamber of the Princess.

'Oh, my darling daughter,' the King exclaimed joyously.

The Queen sat at the Princess's bedside and shook the hand of the handsome young man. 'So this is your Prince! Fine sir, I know not where you come from, or how you might have come to us—but you are meant to be here. We can never thank you enough.'

The King ordered his servants to prepare the castle for a feast grand enough to feed the hunger of a hundred years. While it was being prepared, the Prince and Princess talked without pausing for a moment, and love blossomed in their hearts. Before very long they were married. Two kingdoms came together as one with the young couple as King and Queen, ruling generously over a happy people who would forever believe in magic.

Jack And The Beanstalk

There was once a poor widow, and Jack was her only son. They had one cow, but it grew old and gave less and less milk. Jack would return from milking with his bucket almost empty.

'I knew this time would come,' sighed the widow.

'What shall we do?' Jack asked.

His mother wrung her hands. 'We must try to sell the cow. She is not worth much but we may get enough to buy a goat to milk, or a sow to give us piglets.'

'All right, mother,' Jack said. 'I'll go to the market and sell her. Then we'll see what we can do.'

He set out on the road to the market after breakfast, with

the halter in his hand and the cow clomping along behind him. On the way, he met a stranger who called out a greeting: 'Good morning, young fellow!'

'Good morning,' Jack replied.

'Young fellow, where are you off to?' enquired the man.

'I'm going to the market to sell this cow.' The man came over and looked closely at the cow. 'She's a fine cow,' Jack told him. 'I've milked her every day for years.'

'And she's a little old now, I see,' said the man. 'But I will do you a favour and make your day easy.'

'Are you going to buy her from me?'

'Better than that, young fellow!' The stranger grinned at Jack and winked. 'We can do a little trade.'

'Do you have goats I can take home?' Jack asked. 'Or pigs? Or hens?'

'Better than that,' the man repeated. The man put his hand into his pocket and pulled out a bean. 'I'll swap you that cow for this bean.'

Jack wondered whether the man was mad. 'You are surely joking,' he said. 'Now, excuse me, but I must be on my way.'

'Wait,' the man said. 'This bean is no ordinary bean—it is a *magic* bean.'

Jack rather liked the idea of magic. Many times he had wished for a magic wand to wave away his chores, and to make his mother's life easier. He looked at the man with interest. 'Magic?' he queried. 'What magic can it do?'

'This bean will grow into a towering beanstalk overnight. You will have an endless supply of beans—forever!'

Jack knew that beans were full of goodness, and he knew that a sack of beans could be sold easily at the market. Even so, he was doubtful. 'Really? I have never heard of such beans.'

'That is not surprising,' admitted the man. 'But let us make the trade. If what I say is not true, you can have your cow back.'

This seemed fair, so Jack handed him the cow's halter and took the bean.

While the widow was surprised to see Jack coming back along the road so early, she was pleased that the cow was no longer clomping along behind him. She hastened to meet him.

'Back already, Jack? How much did you get for her?'

'You'll never guess, mother,' Jack replied. Already he was thinking of the money he would make when his first bean crop was harvested.

'Enough to buy a milking goat?' the widow asked.

'Better than that,' Jack said, remembering the man's words.

'Enough to buy another cow?' Now, his mother was excited too.

'Better than that,' laughed Jack. 'I exchanged her for a bean.' Seeing his mother's face fall, he showed her the bean and added: 'It's magic! Plant it, and overnight—'

Anger rose up quickly in the widow. 'What?' she screeched. 'Are you really such a fool? What would your father think? Oh, do I deserve a son who can be conned into giving away our only cow for a bean?'

The widow seized the bean, flung it out the window and sent Jack off to bed. Jack cried until he could cry no more, ashamed that he had let his mother down. Finally, he fell into a deep sleep.

Next morning, the room was unusually dark. Jack dressed and went to the window. Outside, he saw a beanstalk that not only shaded the house but stretched up as far as he could see. The stranger had spoken the truth after all.

Thrilled, Jack climbed through the window and onto the beanstalk. It was like a big plaited ladder, and Jack kept

climbing to discover for himself how high it went. On and on he climbed, right up to the sky.

At the top, he was amazed to find a road. He walked along it and came to an enormous house, where a tall woman was sweeping the front steps. 'Hello,' Jack said, tired and hungry after his climb but eager to meet someone who lived in the sky. 'I've come from far below. Would you be so kind as to spare me a little snack?'

'You want a snack?' the woman chortled. 'You'll become a snack yourself if you stay long around here. My husband is an ogre and there's nothing he finds tastier than boys on toast. Get off home before he sees you!'

The woman's smile made Jack think she was teasing, so he kept on. 'Really and truly,' he said, 'I've had nothing to eat since yesterday morning. If I'm going to die of hunger, I may as well be spread over your husband's toast.'

'What a bold boy,' laughed the ogre's wife. 'If you're willing to risk it, come inside.'

She took Jack to the kitchen and gave him some bread and cheese. While he was eating at her enormous table, a loud thumping was heard and the house began to tremble. 'Oh dear, it's him,' cried the woman, no longer smiling. 'Quick!

Hide in here,' she said, bundling Jack into the oven just as the ogre came in.

The ogre was gigantic. He unhitched three goats from his belt and threw them on the table. 'Wife, cook these for my lunch.' Then he paused for a moment, sniffing the air, and continued:

Fee-fi-fo-fum,
I smell the blood of an Englishman,
Be he alive, or be he dead,
I'll grind his bones to make my bread.

'You're dreaming, dear,' said his wife, 'or perhaps you smell the scraps of the last little boy you ate. Now, let me make you a lovely stew from these goats.'

As soon as the ogre was gone, the woman whispered to Jack, 'Wait there until he has eaten—he always has a little sleep then.'

Soon Jack was listening to the ogre as he slurped and burped his way through a huge lunch. Upon finishing, the ogre stomped over to a locked cupboard and took out two bags, each clinking and jangling with gold. He emptied one of them on to the table and began counting his riches. As he did so, his head began to nod. When he began to snore, the whole house shook again.

Jack opened the oven and looked around. The woman was nowhere to be seen. He crept past the ogre and, grabbing the unopened bag of gold, slipped outside. Off he ran. When he came to the beanstalk, Jack dropped the bag of gold and it fell straight into his mother's garden. He climbed down after it

and showed his mother the gold. The widow danced around joyfully.

'Wasn't I right about the beans?' Jack crowed. 'They really were magical!'

After many months, however, the gold ran out. Although the beanstalk provided Jack and his mother with an endless supply of beans, Jack made up his mind to again try his luck at the top of the beanstalk. Up and up he climbed, till at last he reached the road that led to the big house. The ogre's wife was outside tending her garden.

'Kind woman,' Jack said, as bold as brass, 'do you think you could again spare me something to eat?'

'Go away!' said the woman. 'You escaped my husband last time, but you won't be so lucky twice.'

Jack was by now a master of tricks. 'Some gold coins went missing on the day I came here, and I want to tell you what I saw. Right now, I'm so hungry I can hardly speak. Please, give me something to eat.'

Curious about what Jack had to say, the ogre's wife took him inside and gave him something to eat. But it was almost the ogre's lunchtime, and they soon heard the thump-thump of his footsteps.

Jack knew exactly what to do. With the woman's help, he climbed into the oven. The ogre sniffed the air, and began to snarl:

Fee-fi-fo-fum,
I smell the blood of an Englishman,
Be he alive, or be he dead,
I'll grind his bones to make my bread.

'You're dreaming, dear,' said his wife, serving him a vast spread of five roasted lambs.

'*Fee-fi-fo-fum,*' said the ogre when he had finished. 'Wife, bring me the hen that lays the golden eggs.'

Jack did not imagine the ogre could be serious, but the woman brought in a hen and the ogre ordered it to lay. Sure enough, it produced an egg of solid gold. Soon the ogre rested his head and began to snore loudly.

Jack's heart thumped. If he could only take that hen to his mother, he thought, they would never want for money again. He waited until the woman was gone before creeping on tiptoe toward the hen. As he seized it, it clucked and woke the ogre.

'*Fee-fi-fo-fum*!' the giant roared.

Jack ran and the ogre lumbered after him, making thunder

rumble across the sky. When they reached the beanstalk, the ogre was surprised to see Jack disappear into the clouds below. Jack climbed down the beanstalk for dear life, with the hen pinned under one arm. The ogre watched, uncertain whether he should risk his great weight on such a ladder.

Then he swung himself on to the beanstalk. '*Fee-fi-fo-fum,*' he growled, becoming even angrier as he clambered slowly after the more nimble Jack.

Down below, the widow had come outside to look up at the thunderous clouds. She saw Jack on the swaying beanstalk.

'Mother!' Jack cried. 'Bring me the axe! Be quick!'

The widow rushed to fetch the axe. When she returned, she gaped in horror. The ogre could now be seen below the clouds, and she heard his terrible chant:

Fee-fi-fo-fum,

I smell the blood of an Englishman!

Jack jumped down, handed the hen to his mother and got hold of the axe. He chopped frantically at the beanstalk. It swayed more violently, and the ogre stopped to see what was happening. He bellowed frightfully as Jack gave a mighty chop and the beanstalk began to topple over. The ogre fell heavily with it, shaking the land for miles around. He had breathed his last.

'You rash young fool,' Jack's mother chided. 'What risks you have taken—for a common hen!'

'Ah-ha!' chirped Jack. 'This hen may look common, but it lays eggs that are not so common.'

Once they were inside, he set the hen on the table. 'Lay,' he commanded. The hen cackled and fussed, but did as it was told. The widow could not believe her eyes.

'Lay,' she told the hen, and it laid a second golden egg for them. She threw her arms around Jack and held him close. 'My brave, clever boy! Your father would be proud of you. We will grow rich on this hen, and I shall find a princess for you to wed.'

Jack laughed happily. 'Princesses can wait,' he told her. 'For now, all I'd like is a big bowl of your delicious bean soup.'

The Ugly Duckling

Mother Duck sat on her nest in the shade of a tree. She was tired of the long wait for her eggs to hatch, for she did not have many visitors. The farmer's other ducks preferred to swim on the pond than sit gossiping with her.

Finally, one eggshell cracked and a little beak made a hole large enough for the little duckling to push through. As it lay puffing and panting, another egg began to hatch, and then some more.

'Peep, peep,' went the ducklings, quickly getting to know each other. 'How big the world is!'

'Quack, quack,' said Mother Duck, proud of her little ones but noticing that the largest egg had not yet begun to crack. She seated herself on the nest again and sighed.

An old duck had heard the peep-peep of the ducklings and

came waddling up to Mother Duck's nest. 'Such a beautiful brood,' she said. 'Are they all out now?'

'Not yet,' Mother Duck replied. 'I have one very big egg left.'

'Let me see it,' said the old duck. 'The farmer once put a turkey's egg under me. Perhaps he has played that trick on you.'

Mother Duck moved aside and the old duck scoffed. 'It is far too big to be yours. Don't bother with it—it's a turkey's egg, to be sure.'

'I'll sit just a little while longer,' said Mother Duck. 'Let's see what happens.'

'Please yourself then,' said the old duck. 'But be warned—you'll never succeed in teaching a turkey chick how to swim. I tried but failed completely.' The old duck waddled away.

At last the egg broke, and a young one emerged. It was a dirty grey colour with a black beak, and much larger than the others. Mother Duck stared at this ugly duckling, wondering if it really might be a turkey. 'We'll soon find out when we swim on the pond,' she thought.

After the ducklings had rested a while, Mother Duck led them to the pond. In they went, one after the other. The ugly one did not hesitate, and swam without difficulty like the others.

'Well, he can't be a turkey,' Mother Duck told herself. 'How well he uses his legs, and how upright he holds himself!'

Off she went to introduce her ducklings to the farmer's other ducks, who were watching from the far side of the

pond. Among them was a duck of high breeding. Her golden feathers had won the farmer prizes at country shows, and she was really rather snooty.

'Be on your best behaviour,' Mother Duck quacked to the little ones swimming in her wake.

The ducklings did as they were told, but the duck with the golden feathers was not impressed. 'Another brood—as if there were not enough of us already! Look at that big one. He's such an ugly-looking creature, very grubby-looking for one so freshly hatched.'

One of the other ducks, keen to impress the snooty one, flew out and bit the ugly duckling on the neck.

'Leave him alone,' protested Mother Duck. 'He's not doing any harm. He may not be cute, but he can swim even better than the others. He'll grow up strong—then you'll be sorry.'

In spite of Mother Duck's words, the farmyard ducks gave the ugly duckling a very hard time. The Ugly Duckling—for this became his name—was bitten and chased and teased, not only by the ducks but also by the farmer's hens and turkeys. Even his brothers and sisters were unkind, so he spent hours swimming in the pond alone.

The Ugly Duckling was so miserable that, at the first opportunity, he escaped the farm and made his way across the fields. Birds flew away as he approached, and mice scurried out of sight. 'They're afraid of me because I'm ugly,' he thought.

Eventually he came to a river, feeling worn-out and sorrowful. He slept a while and, when he awoke, found himself surrounded by a flock of wild ducks.

'What sort of duck are you?' they enquired in a chorus of quacks.

'An exceptionally ugly one,' pronounced one splendid drake.

'But who cares? As long as he doesn't plan to marry into our family!'

The Ugly Duckling had no thoughts of marriage—all he wanted was to swim on the river, and to poke around and eat his fill of worms.

After two days by the river, he was joined by a rowdy gaggle of wild geese. The Ugly Duckling had never seen a goose before and hoped he could make some friends. 'You and your family are quite large for ducks,' he said to one young fellow. 'And I was the biggest duckling ever seen in my farmyard. Do you think we may be alike?'

'I do beg your pardon,' replied the goose. 'But I am not a duck. I'm a *goose* and very proud of it. You are far too ugly to be a goose, so you mustn't waste any more time thinking about it.'

Sadly the Ugly Duckling retreated, hiding in the rushes by the river's edge. He'd only been lying there a few minutes when he heard a commotion. There was the sound of dogs, whining and yelping with excitement. The wild geese flew up, honking in panic.

Bang. Bang-bang. Hunters fired and two geese fell into the river. Gun smoke floated across the water and dogs bounded among the rushes. The Ugly Duckling was terrified. A big dog appeared beside him and thrust his nose very close before plunging into the river to retrieve one of the fallen geese.

The Ugly Duckling sighed. 'Maybe I should be *thankful* for being so ugly. Even a dog will not bite me.'

When all became quiet, several hours passed before the poor creature dared move. Finally he hurried off, alarmed now by a rising storm. Coming to a cottage, he took shelter on its veranda.

The woman who lived in this cottage was old and very short-sighted. Her closest companion was a cat, and she lived

on the eggs of a very plump hen. After the storm, the woman found the Ugly Duckling outside her door and mistook it for a fully grown duck, thinking it had strayed in the storm.

'What luck!' she exclaimed. 'Now I'll have duck eggs as well as the eggs from my hen.'

The Ugly Duckling was taken in and fed, but naturally could not produce any eggs. The hen teased him cruelly, and the cat soon joined in. 'So, you cannot lay eggs. Can you purr, or warm the lap of the woman who feeds you? Can you catch mice?'

The Ugly Duckling sat in a corner, feeling very low-spirited. As the days passed, he thought more and more about water,

and felt a great desire to swim. Having no one else to talk to, he told the hen.

'How foolish you are,' replied the hen. 'If you could do something useful, you wouldn't have time for such crazy thoughts.'

'But it's nice to swim about on water,' insisted the Ugly Duckling. 'And it's refreshing to duck your head and dive down to the bottom.'

'Fun indeed!' said the hen. 'Ask the cat. He is the cleverest animal I know, so just ask him if he'd like to swim. I know what answer you will get.'

The Ugly Duckling sighed. 'You don't understand me,' he said.

'We don't understand you? *Who* can understand you, I wonder? If you want my advice, learn to lay eggs as quickly as possible.'

'Since that seems impossible, I think I must go out into the world again,' said the Ugly Duckling.

'Then go,' said the hen, and the Ugly Duckling left the cottage and found water on which it could swim and dive. By now, however, winter was approaching. Clouds hung low in the sky. The water grew colder every day, and the Ugly Duckling felt lonelier than ever.

One afternoon, he heard the beating of wings and saw a most spectacular sight. From somewhere nearby, a flock of white swans was taking to the sky. He had never seen birds with such graceful necks and feathers so dazzling. On powerful wings they set off for warmer countries beyond the sea.

Watching, the Ugly Duckling felt a little peculiar. He stretched his neck upward and let out a cry so strange that it surprised even himself. He did not know what the big, beautiful birds were, and he didn't know where they were going. He only knew that he'd never forget them.

As winter set in, snow fell and the water froze. No longer

able to swim, the Ugly Duckling huddled with his head under a wing. He would surely have died had a man not passed and taken pity on him, bundling the feeble bird under his arm and carrying it home.

After the Ugly Duckling had eaten and was revived by the warmth of the kitchen, the man's children began to play

with him. They played so roughly that they bruised him and plucked his young feathers. He flapped and landed in the milk pan, and the man's wife then struck at him with her tongs. They all tried to catch him, but the door was open and the Ugly Duckling escaped.

He sheltered in a dark cave. It was dry inside and there were snails to eat, but the winter was long and lonely. How he

survived it, he would never know—but eventually it passed and the Ugly Duckling emerged into the warm spring sun. He grazed on grass shoots and found worms emerging from mud that had long been frozen over.

One day, the Ugly Duckling stretched his wings and, feeling new strength, flapped them against his sides. His feet left the ground and he discovered, for the first time, the pleasure of flight. He flew until he saw below a most delightful garden. Apple trees were in blossom and a pretty stream ran into a clear blue lake.

Three majestic swans were gliding across the smooth water. The Ugly Duckling recognised the birds, but now the sight of them made him feel sorry for himself. 'Why must I live like this?' he thought. 'Ugly and unwanted from the time I left my egg, I will never find company, let alone have such grace.'

Overcome with sorrow, the Ugly Duckling decided to rest on the lake. 'If those royal birds attack me,' he thought, 'they will probably be powerful enough to kill me.' But he didn't care. A long life of being pecked and chased and starved in winter seemed even more frightful.

He flew to the water and swam towards the swans. They rushed to meet him with outstretched wings. The Ugly Duckling bent his head to the surface of the water and waited for the pain and injury their beaks would surely cause.

But what did he see in the clear water below? His own image—no longer a dull, overgrown duck, but an elegant and handsome swan. The other swans swam round the newcomer and nuzzled his neck with gentle, welcoming beaks.

Children came into the garden and threw bread into the water. 'There's a new one,' cried the youngest. 'Another swan has come, the most beautiful of them all!' The children ran to their parents, clapping their hands and shouting their news.

The Ugly Duckling didn't know what to think or do—the surprise of learning that he was neither ugly nor even a duck was simply too great. Slowly, however, happiness warmed his heart—not because he was beautiful but because he belonged, and was loved. He rustled his feathers, curved his slender neck and cried for joy.

Cinderella

Long ago, a beautiful girl lived with her father, a nobleman. She was a good and thoughtful girl who reminded her father of his dear wife, who had died during childbirth. Eventually, the man took a second wife, hoping she would help raise his daughter and not knowing of the woman's heartlessness. The woman's own twin daughters were spoiled, selfish and nasty, and would make their stepsister's life miserable.

The wedding was hardly over before the girl's father needed to travel to a faraway kingdom. Immediately, the stepmother set the girl to do all the work of the house. She washed the dishes, swept the floors, and scrubbed the bath, basins and sinks. She was given only rags to dress herself in, while the twins wore the prettiest of dresses. Even worse, the girl was forced to sleep in the cellar on a tattered straw mattress while her stepsisters slept in the room that had once been hers. Winters were bitterly cold, and she was sometimes seen warming her hands over the coals of fires that had kept her stepsisters warm during the night.

'Look at her,' said one of the twins. 'Her best friends are coals and cinders.'

'We'll call her Cinderella,' laughed the other—and so they did.

In spite of everything, Cinderella did not complain. She believed that things would change when her father returned. In the meantime, she spoke politely and worked hard.

It so happened that the nobleman was still away when the King's son decided to host a grand ball. He invited the young lords and ladies from the finest households in the land. Rumours spread quickly, and the biggest of them all was that the Prince was ready to take a bride. Cinderella's stepsisters spent entire days discussing the clothes and shoes they might wear, as well as rehearsing their manners. Both were convinced that they could charm the Prince into marrying them, just as their mother had charmed Cinderella's father.

Meanwhile, the stepmother kept Cinderella hard at work

with household chores, and forced them to iron the twins' many new clothes. Sometimes Cinderella's stepsisters asked her opinion on clothes and colour combinations, for they considered her dress sense to be excellent. Cinderella offered her views graciously, and sometimes even offered to brush and style the twins' hair.

Finally, the day of the ball arrived. Cinderella's stepsisters were beside themselves with excitement. They waited in the parlour for their carriage to arrive, dressed to the nines and laden with jewellery. Cinderella caught sight of them as she swept the hall.

'Oh!' she exclaimed. 'You look stunning! Our Prince will have his breath taken away, and he will not know which one of you to dance with!'

'You must wish you were coming too,' said one twin. The other laughed, as if that thought was too ridiculous for words. 'Unfortunately, housemaids are not allowed,' the first twin added, and her sister laughed again.

'I have no such wish,' sighed Cinderella. 'I would be laughed at, just as you are laughing now.'

But when her stepsisters had left, Cinderella began to sob. In her heart, she longed to wear a lovely dress and to be swept around the dance floor at the Prince's ball. She wept and wept until, suddenly, she sensed the presence of someone else in the room. Fearing her stepmother, Cinderella looked up to find a striking woman, radiant and smiling kindly at her.

'I am your Fairy Godmother,' the woman said. 'It pains me

to see you so very sad. I know your true wishes.'

Cinderella did not know what to say. She was certain she was dreaming.

'Go to the garden and bring me a pumpkin,' the Fairy Godmother instructed. The habit of doing as she was told was strong, and she carried out the task like a sleepwalker. She placed the pumpkin on the table.

'Fetch me a knife and spoon,' said the Fairy Godmother. When Cinderella did so, she continued, 'You do want to go to that ball, am I right?'

Cinderella nodded and the Fairy Godmother began hollowing out the pumpkin. When she finished, she touched Cinderella lightly on the shoulder with her magic wand. Suddenly, she was wearing a most spectacular gown and some lovely jewellery. On her feet was a delicate pair of glass slippers.

'Now I am dressed for the ball,' Cinderella said. 'And I am most grateful to you, Fairy Godmother. But still I cannot go, for there is no coach to carry me.'

The Fairy Godmother picked up the shell of the pumpkin and carried it outside. She waved her wand and it was instantly

transformed into a golden coach. Cinderella was astonished.

'But who will drive it?' she wondered aloud. She need not have worried. Already her Fairy Godmother was waving her wand and turning mice into a team of majestic horses, and a rat into a coachman.

'So,' the Fairy Godmother said, 'off you go! The night is young and you must make the most of it. But a word of warning—take care to return before midnight. The spells I have cast will expire at the stroke of twelve, and a hollow pumpkin will get you nowhere.'

When the golden coach arrived at the palace, it was thought that a princess had arrived. Word quickly reached the Prince, and he dashed out to escort her into the ballroom. He was immediately enchanted by Cinderella's beauty, and her entrance on his arm caused a sensation. The fiddlers stopped playing and the dancing stopped as everyone turned to stare.

'Oh, how lovely she is!' murmured the lords.

'Such style!' exclaimed the ladies.

Cinderella's makeover was such that even her stepsisters failed to recognise her. 'Look at those jewels!' said one. 'And her exquisite shoes!' said the other.

Cinderella danced so gracefully that everybody's admiration of her increased even further. When Cinderella greeted her stepsisters by name, they wondered who this princess might be, not imagining for a moment that she was the girl who mopped and cleaned their rooms. Cinderella was bright and witty with the Prince, and neither of them ate when a lavish feast was served, so absorbed were they in conversation.

After dancing some more, the two were again talking gaily when Cinderella heard the clock strike eleven forty-five. She had completely lost track of time. Her heart racing, she curtseyed to the Prince and made her way through the packed ballroom as quickly as she could. The Prince hesitated for a moment, quite taken aback. Then he charged after her. He reached the door just in time to see Cinderella climbing urgently into her golden carriage, not even stopping to retrieve a glass slipper that fell off in her haste. As the carriage disappeared into the night, he picked up the slipper and cradled it, lost in love for all to see.

Cinderella had not quite reached home when she found herself on foot without coach or horses in her old, shabby

clothes, with nothing to show for her night out but a single glass slipper. Just looking at it made her breathless with longing to see the Prince again. She hid the glass slipper among her possessions in the cellar where she slept.

When the twins arrived home from the ball, they seemed a little crestfallen that the Prince had taken little notice of them, but could not stop talking about the princess who had won his attention.

'He picked up her slipper as if it was an injured nightingale,' said one. 'And he did little else but gaze upon it for the remainder of the evening.'

'Oh, the agony on his face!' sighed the other.

Soon, Cinderella heard that the King had commanded his men to find the owner of the glass slipper so that his heartbroken son could marry her. They were to search high and low, and would not rest until they found the bright and lovely girl the slipper had so clearly been made for. While Cinderella's heart sang to know that the Prince was so very much in love with her, she was also worried that she may not be given a chance to try on her lost slipper. After all, she thought, nobody knew she had been to the ball.

The King's men began their quest by trying the slipper on princesses in neighbouring kingdoms, and then duchesses. Finally they proceeded to the homes of the kingdom's noblemen and arrived at Cinderella's father's house.

First one stepsister tried on the slipper, then the other. No matter how hard they tried, they could not make it fit. 'Oh dear,' moaned one loudly, 'I fear my feet have swollen horribly since the ball.'

'My good lady,' replied the most senior of the King's men, 'the bones in your feet cannot swell, and sadly for you, it is those which are too large for this slipper.'

'Sir, may I try?' Cinderella's voice was small. Her heart was pounding.

The twins began to laugh and ridicule her, but the man looked attentively at her. He saw that she was very beautiful, even dressed in rags.

'The instruction I have been given is to try the slipper on all maidens, without exception,' he said. 'Besides, what harm can it do?'

Cinderella's stepsisters watched in astonishment as the man motioned for Cinderella to sit as he fitted the shoe. It wrapped her foot closely, like a wax mould.

'I have the other one right here,' Cinderella said. She took it from her pocket and held it up.

At that very moment, the Fairy Godmother appeared. The King's men gasped. One of the stepsisters almost fainted, and was only saved from a fall by her twin.

'Look at them,' the Fairy Godmother laughed. 'Poor folk—they've never seen a Fairy Godmother before!' With that, she tapped Cinderella's head with her magic wand. Cinderella's clothes were transformed once again, matching the elegance of the glass slippers. The King's men bowed to her at once.

Cinderella's stepsisters now saw in her the beautiful person they had seen at the ball. They knelt at her feet, begging her to forgive them for all the meanness they had shown to her in her father's absence. Cinderella pulled them up and embraced them.

'We are family,' she said tenderly. 'I only ask that we love and respect each other as sisters from this day forward. We must all let bygones be bygones.'

The King's men escorted Cinderella to the palace. The young Prince could barely contain his joy. He found her more charming than ever, and sent out his men to find Cinderella's father and bring him home. Puzzled at first, her father was finally delighted, and gladly granted Cinderella's hand in marriage.

Cinderella held no grudge against her stepsisters, and they were soon married to two great lords of the King's court. They lived happily ever after in the palace with the Prince and his beautiful Princess.

Squeel
Squeel
Squeel

The Three Little Pigs

Once there were three little pigs. They were full of energy and played rough and tumble games, with a lot of squealing. They ate fast, licking their plates clean and always wanting seconds.

Their poor mother knew that they needed more than she could give. It was hard to keep them in her little old house. Sadly, she told the three little pigs that it was time to become *big* little pigs. They would need to go out bravely and take care of themselves.

Off the three little pigs went, each with a lunchbox packed with treats. Down the path they trotted, and along a big road. Soon they met a man on his way to market with a donkey piled high with straw.

One of the pigs had an idea. 'Good sir,' he said, 'would you like to swap one of my yummy treats for your straw? I want to make a house.'

The man was hungry, so he agreed. The first little pig said goodbye to his brothers and got busy, quickly building a house of straw.

Further along the road, the two little pigs saw a woman stacking branches and sticks to burn when winter came. 'Ah ha!' thought the second little pig. 'Those sticks are just what I need to build my house.'

'Please madam,' the pig began, 'I will give you half of these treats for half of your sticks. I need to make a house.'

The woman looked at the little pig and felt slightly sorry for him. 'You may keep your treats,' she said, 'but take as many sticks as you need.'

The second little pig tied a huge bundle of sticks with rope and dragged it away to build his house. He felt lucky, and worked hard to make a house he could be proud of.

The third little pig continued on his way. He imagined how nice it would be to sit down in the sunshine and eat his treats —but he knew he better not. What if he needed them later, to exchange for some straw or sticks and build a house like his brothers? Moments later, the pig saw a man driving a horse and cart. The cart was overloaded with bricks and the pig thought, 'Ah ha!' He waved at the man and asked him to stop.

'I have only these yummy treats to give you. Would you be kind enough to let me have some bricks?'

The man had been worried that the load of bricks was too heavy for his horse to pull all the way to the village. He looked into the third little pig's lunchbox and his eyes widened. 'Very well,' the man nodded. 'Show me where you'd like me to unload some for you.'

All the little pigs worked hard to build their houses. That night, each one of them was exhausted.

The first little pig was getting ready for bed when he heard a wolf outside. The wolf's stomach was rumbling loudly. Little pigs, he knew, could be scrumptious little meals.

'Little pig, little pig, let me come in,' the wolf growled.

In his new straw house, the first little pig shook with fear. 'Oh no!' he replied. 'Not by the hair of my chinny chin chin.'

The wolf only laughed. 'Then I'll huff, and I'll puff, and I'll blow your house in.'

So he huffed, and he puffed, and he blew the house in. In a few moments he had eaten up the little pig and was setting off to look for another tasty bite.

When the wolf saw the second little pig's house of sticks, he licked his lips eagerly. Inside, the little pig was munching on one of his mother's lunchbox treats.

'Little pig, little pig, let me come in,' the wolf growled.

'Never!' said the pig. 'Not by the hair of my chinny chin chin!'

'Then I'll huff, and I'll puff, and I'll blow your house in,' came the voice of the wolf.

He huffed, and he puffed, and he huffed a little more. Finally, he blew the house in. In the blink of an eye, the second little pig became the wolf's second meal of the night.

The third little pig was tired and hungry after building his house of bricks. Part of him wished he hadn't given the man with the horse and cart all he had to eat—but if he hadn't, he wouldn't have his nice brick house, complete with a fireplace to keep him warm.

By now the wolf was feeling rather full. Even so, he knocked on the little pig's door.

'Little pig, little pig, let me come in.'

'Not by the hair of my chinny chin chin!'

'Then I'll huff, and I'll puff, and I'll blow your house in.'

The wolf huffed, and he puffed. He puffed and he huffed. Then he huffed and puffed again. Soon he realised that huffing and puffing were useless. He could *not* blow the third little pig's house down.

'I shall need to be patient,' he thought, 'but I will eat this pig tomorrow.' The wolf called out in his most charming voice: 'You win, little pig—but I'm sure you must be hungry. I know where you can find a nice field of turnips.'

'Where?' asked the little pig.

'Not far from the bend in the river,' the wolf said. 'I can take you there in the morning and you can collect some for dinner. Be ready at seven o'clock.'

'Very well,' the little pig told the wolf, 'I will be ready.'

Next morning, the wolf returned to the brick house. To his surprise he found that the little pig had left at six o'clock and found the turnip field near the river. Turnips were already stewing over the little pig's fire. The wolf was annoyed, but again spoke kindly to the little pig. 'I know where there is a nice apple tree,' he said. 'Do you like apples?'

The little pig did like apples—very much! 'Where is this tree?' he asked.

'It's on a hill near the milking shed,' replied the wolf. 'I will come for you at six o'clock in the morning. Be sure to wait for me and I will help you collect some apples.'

The little pig woke at five o'clock and hurried off in the direction of the milking shed. Soon he saw the apple tree. His bucket was almost full when he saw the wolf coming up the hill.

'Little pig, little pig—you are always so early!'

The wolf looked angry. Although the little pig was frightened, he called out to the wolf.

'These are such sweet apples,' said the little pig. 'Here—try one!'

The little pig threw an apple in the direction of the wolf. It rolled past the wolf and down the hill. As the wolf turned to go after it, the pig jumped down and raced home as fast as his legs would carry him.

Next day, the wolf came to the third little pig's brick house again. 'Little pig, I will forgive you for your rudeness yesterday. We can still be friends. There is a fair in the village this afternoon. Shall we go?'

'Oh yes,' said the pig. 'What time should I get ready?'

'At three,' said the wolf. 'And remember, fairs are much more fun when you go with friends.'

The little pig thought this was probably true, but knew the wolf should not be trusted. He went to the fair two hours earlier than arranged and had returned home by the time the wolf arrived.

Now the wolf was furious. Three attempts to trick the little pig had failed and three times the wolf had been tricked by the pig. Each time the wolf had become hungrier.

'You are the most annoying little pig I have ever met,' he boomed. 'I will eat you if it is the last thing I do!'

The little pig saw immediately that the wolf's rage would make him do something foolish. Sure enough, the wolf set about climbing to the roof so that he could slide down the chimney.

The little pig lit a blazing fire and set a big pot of water to boil. The wolf struggled, groaning and growling, all the way to the top of the house. Finally, he climbed into the chimney.

'Dinner time, little pig,' the wolf snarled as he hurtled down the chimney.

FAIR

'Dinner time, big wolf!' the little pig said, as he watched the wolf plunge into his pot of boiling water. The little pig covered the pot with a lid and wondered what wolf soup tasted like.

Little Pig lived happily ever after as he was never troubled by the wolf again.